Read Our Story – Have Fun Making It Your Own

Adventures of
Princess Isabella

The Leprechaun

Authors:
Linda Romblom & Isabella Walker

Illustrators:
Isabella Walker & Linda Romblom

AuthorHouse™
1663 Liberty Drive
Bloomington, IN 47403
www.authorhouse.com
Phone: 1 (800) 839-8640

Published by AuthorHouse 02/25/2017

ISBN: 978-1-5246-7361-1 (sc)
ISBN: 978-1-5246-7360-4 (e)

Print information available on the last page.

This book is printed on acid-free paper.

authorHOUSE®

Interactive Personalized Storybook
Simple as 1 - 2 - 3
...and A - B - C

1 - Read the Story Together

2 - Discuss the Story (See Questions)

3 - Write Your Own Story (See Template)

    A - Change the Names to Personalize
       Lead Character, Supporting People, Animals

    B - Illustrate Your Story in Space Provided
       Use Colored Pencils, Crayons, and Markers

    C - Omit Any Parts You Don't Want in Your Story
       and Add Anything Else You Like

An Adventure in Creative Story Telling!

Introduction

This book began as bedtime stories created by a grandmother (Linda Romblom) shared with her granddaughter (Isabella Walker) who became the leading character, Princess Isabella, in this great adventure. Her family members, and friends play supporting roles and she named animals in the story as it was told.

As Isabella grew and became interested in reading and drawing, these special times between grandmother and granddaughter expanded into creating this book.

Now you too can share the magic using this fun interactive storybook. Begin with our story in the front of the book, and then personalize it using the template provided in the back. Child authors play the leading role as Princess or Prince with their selected supporting cast and assortment of animals that they name. Use whatever medium you like to illustrate the scenes in the space provided.

Remember that the quality of the picture is secondary to the quality of the time spent together in the creative process. Isabella, the primary illustrator of this book is 7 years old. She used pencil, markers, and crayons. Occasionally, she would find a picture, usually on her iPad, of something she was trying to draw, like a German Shepard dog and her pups, or a leprechaun. At one point Isabella encouraged Grammie Linda to try her hand at drawing instead of just coloring. See if you can tell where that began. Hint: it is the page where the leprechaun should have been smaller or Isabella bigger.

At the end of the story you will find a series of questions to guide discussion about the story. Whether at bedtime, or even in a classroom setting, the goal is to get kids thinking deeper about ideas presented in the story, and then connecting these thoughts with their life experiences. The questions deal with experiencing the story, cultural awareness, character, problem-solving, and a quest for learning.

This book is a product of love shared. May the sharing of it continue to expand, the love of learning, and, the learning of loving, to those who participate in the experience.

ENJOY!

Once upon a time, long, long ago, in a land far away, there lived a beautiful princess named Isabella. She lived in a castle, high on a hill, with her father, King Jeffrey, her mother, Queen Elizabeth, and her little brother, Prince Elijah. Often the Queen Mother, Linda, came to visit and such adventures they had together.'

Isabella had dark brown hair with just a little bit of curl that danced in the wind. Usually she kept it tied back, especially when horseback riding. Her eyes were dark brown, almost black, and had the most amazing ability to show how she felt on the inside.

On a bright sunny morning, her eyes twinkled with delight as she took a deep breath and inhaled the sweet smell of lilac bushes that grew along the path to the stable. It was a grand morning for a ride in the country, and Queen Elizabeth said she could ride as far as the creek, but needed to be home in time for lunch.

As Isabella neared the stable she saw Mr. Jimmy giving the horses grain over the fence. The horses seemed as happy with the sunshine and fresh air as was the little princess.

"Which of your beauties will you be riding today, your highness." asked Jimmy. They were indeed beauties! She preferred the two white horses, Chance and Naomi, for a carriage ride, because they not only looked elegant together, but worked well as a team, being well paired for the pull. Today she selected Sophia, a light brown mare, who was gentle, yet enjoyed a good run.

Mr. Jimmy headed toward the barn to get a saddle. Isabella joined him to check on their German Shepard dog, Reese, and her pups. There was a sweet smell of hay mixed with other barn smells, some, not so sweet! Light coming through the windows showed a speckled array of dust in the air.

"Here Reese, come puppies," called Isabella. As she turned the corner near the last stall she saw why Reese did not come when called. Like the good mama dog that she was, her first duty was to provide breakfast for her growing family. Reclined in the hay the little fur balls were lined up and happily nursing. Isabella snuggled down with them and gently petted Reese. The puppies eyes had opened just two days ago and their little faces were so sweet. The littlest one, Buddy, was having trouble finding a spot to nurse among his brothers and sisters, so Isabella helped him by moving Lucky over to make room.

"Now that's better. You must learn to share" she said.

Just then Jimmy called, "Ready when you are Princess."

"Thanks Jimmy, for your help," said Isabella as she put her foot in the stirrup to get on Sophia. The style of her riding pants looked a bit funny with their pouched-out sides, but they were well designed for comfort in the saddle. She headed down the dusty road between the two rows of huge oak trees. The trees were so tall and broad that their branches came together high overhead, shading her from the bright morning sun. It was a peaceful ride, interrupted only by the chatter of two chipmunks chasing each other about the branches of a tree. A robin bounced in the short grass, pecking the ground for worms. She could hear a chorus of other song birds in the area, but really didn't know which bird made which song.

"That would be worth learning someday," Isabella thought to herself. But for today she was just happy to be right here, enjoying the sights and the sounds of it all.

Princess Isabella was glad to feel the full warmth again of the sunshine as she left the trees and entered a meadow. It was like being on a sea, as the grass waved in the wind like waves on an ocean. Sprinkled with an array of wildflowers in hues of blue, yellow and white; the beauty of the meadow beckoned her to become a part of it. The wind lifted her hair and Sophia's mane. At the same second, both felt the need for speed. They raced across the meadow with a delicious feeling of freedom and joy.

Going from a smooth gallop to a trot was bouncy so Isabella held tight to Sophia's mane.

"Good girl," Princess Isabella whispered as they slowed to a walk near the bank of the river. She got off her horse and tied Sophia to some large bushes nearby where there was lots of thick grass to munch.

Down the little hill near the water were several large flat rocks that began on the land and went out into the water. This was one of Isabella's favorite places. She loved to lay on the rocks in the sunshine and dangle her toes in the water. It was the perfect spot to study the clouds and imagine what each shape looked like and then watch it change. She had spent many hours there imagining with her grandmother, known to most people as "the queen mother," but to Isabella she was "Grammie Linda."

As Isabella settled down into her rock, she could almost hear Grandma's voice saying, "be careful near the water." "*I hope Grammie Linda comes for a visit again soon,*" she thought with a smile. "*I miss the fun times we have together, and when we get the giggles, and she snorts.*"

There were lots of clouds in the sky and the young princess identified several cloud creatures including, a fish, rabbit, and bird. The fish was only its mouth, and the rabbit instead of hopping away just made a big slur and was gone. She could almost hear the bird chirping. No, that sound was not bird like, it was more of a clicking sound.

Princess Isabella sat upright to really listen to the unusual sound. Sure enough, it was like "click, click, click." What was it? Where did it come from? It was too regular to be a twig breaking, and not the kind of fast regular tapping one hears from a woodpecker. What could it be?

She got up and climbed the bank near the tree and listened. The sound could hardly be heard. So, she went back to the edge of the water. Yes, the sound was louder again there. She started to walk along the shore to her right and the sound disappeared, so she turned and walked in the other direction, and ...yes...definitely, it was getting louder! Her heart was racing with excitement.

Oh no, it stopped! (The sound that is, not her heart.) She stopped too, waiting, and listening. There seemed to be another sound now. Almost like a hum. Not like a bee would hum, or even a humming bird kind of sound, but almost like a voice far away humming. Ever so quietly she crept forward. Yes, it was getting louder.

By this time Princess Isabella had traveled quite a distance along the bank of the river. It was more like a stream at this point. There were rocks and a big log so that anyone could even cross to the other side. And that's exactly what she decided to do. She planned her path carefully, which rock each step would take, until using the log to cross the little stream. She knew that even if she fell in, it was not very deep. Just as she stepped foot on the far side of the river she heard another strange sound. Like someone clearing their throat, and then a little cough. She looked around and at first couldn't see anything unusual. But then she saw him, and unusual only began to describe the sight she saw.

It was no wonder she hadn't seen him right away because he was only a few feet high, and he was dressed in green so blended in with the green grass and bushes. He sat on a rock a few feet away from where she stood and was looking right at her. He was shorter than Isabella's little brother Eli, but was not a child, but a man. His skin was wrinkled and he had a beard. His clothes were different, to say the least. His shoes had gold buckles and the toes came to a point and curled up over his foot. He wore long stockings and short pants, banded just below the knee and held tight with a gold button. He had a vest with a pocket watch and a tailored jacket and top-hat with a brown band and gold buckle that held something green in it. Just as she realized that something was like a clover leaf, the hat started moving.

He tipped it to her and said, "Top of the mornin' to ye lass."

"Oh my," said the little princess, quite in shock. "Who are you?"

He got up from where he sat on the rock, did a deep bow and answered with a poem....

"Why, I'm Patrick, Dennis, Michael O'Shaun
    An Irish elf, called a leprechaun,
  Dressed in green from my head to my toes
    For that is the color of leprechaun clothes.
    .... and just who might ye be,
       Yon pretty wee lassie?
    Are ye gone, and lost from home,
      In these woods, so far to roam?"

"I, ah, ...I am P-Princess I-Isabella" she said with a tremble in her voice. "I heard s-something and c-came looking for the s-sound," she stammered.

The elf pulled on his whiskers and asked, "Aye, what sorta sound then?"

"Oh, it was first a click, click, click sound and then a humming sound," Isabella said, feeling a little more comfortable, now that he wasn't talking in verse anymore. *"He does have a strange accent though"*, she thought to herself.

"Aye, I'm a bettin' what ye heard was me wee hammer a tappin', and I'm likin' to hum to meself whilst workin'. Actually, I was takin' a wee bit of a break from me workin' and just a hummin'."

Princess Isabella thought, *"Yep it must have been him I heard."* Her thoughts were interrupted by hearing him clear his throat again and asking rather formally, "Was 'bout to have a wee bit of lunch lass, would ye share a bit with me then?"

"Oh lunch, Oh, no, I have to be home for lunch!" Isabella said as she turned to leave and then remembered her manners. "Thank you so much for the kind invitation, but I really don't have time today. May I come again another time?"

Isabella glanced up to the sun high in the sky and knew it was close to lunch time. She quickly, but carefully, crossed the tiny river, and ran along the beach until her favorite rocks were in sight. Her horse, Sophia was enjoying the tall grass, but glad when the little princess untied the reigns and swung into the saddle. The ride home was like a race to keep her promise to be home in time for lunch. Queen Elizabeth gave Princess Isabella a lot a freedom for her age because Isabella was responsible. She did her chores, and was careful, and honest and kind. The little Princess knew that if she was not true to her word, to be home in time for lunch, some of the trust and freedom she enjoyed might be taken away. Her little brother Eli, didn't have so much freedom because he was several years younger, and wasn't capable of earning trust yet.

She couldn't help but think of her other invitation. *"How interesting it would be to have lunch with a leprechaun,"* she thought. *"Oh, what if I am late. Surely mom and dad will understand if I tell them about Patrick Dennis Michael O'Shaun."*

Princess Isabella was thankful that Mr. Jimmy was there to care for Sophia when she reached the stables. Her legs carried her swiftly to the castle where she stopped for a quick wash. She really should change clothes, but there probably wasn't time.

Cook gave her a nod saying, "Best hurry dear, there is to be a special guest for lunch."

"Oh no!" thought Isabella, *"Not one of those very prim and proper lords or ladies. I'll be in trouble for wearing my riding clothes."*

As Isabella entered the dining room she saw her mom, Queen Elizabeth, who smiled warmly beaconing her in.

"Whew, that's a relief." thought Isabella.

"You made it back just in time sweetheart," said Queen Elizabeth, "come and be seated." Just as Princess Isabella started to ask about the special guest, who walked in but Queen Mother Linda.

Princess Isabella ran to her with arms outstretched saying, "Oh Grammie Linda, I'm so glad to see you!" Their hugs were always warm and long. Little brother Eli joined in a group hug.

"How long can you stay?" asked Isabella.

"Long enough for some great adventures" was her grandmother's reply with a twinkle in her eye.

After hugs were shared all around, the family settled for lunch. King Jeffrey asked Isabella if she would like to say the blessing. The family held hands and bowed their heads, as the little princess thanked God not only for the food, but also the beautiful day and for her family and friends. Their tasty lunch of ham biscuits, potato salad and applesauce was enjoyed as they visited together. When the conversation got around to what Isabella had been doing that morning, at first she hesitated. But then shared her ride to the rocks, hearing the clicking and following the sounds, and how exciting it was to meet a leprechaun!

King Jeffrey said, "Now Isabella, isn't that the place by the river where you lay and look at the clouds and sometimes fall asleep?"

"Well sometimes," she admitted.

"And don't you think that maybe meeting the leprechaun might have just been a dream?"

"Oh no, daddy," the little princess replied, "He was real. And he even asked me to lunch, but I couldn't stay, because I promised to be home for lunch. ....and he invited me to come back another time.

"Oh, that's nice honey," said her mom with a wink at her dad.

"Grammie Linda, you believe me, don't you?" pleaded Isabella.

"Of course I do sweetheart," she replied, "Do you suppose I could go with you when you go back to see him again."

"Oh, yes Grammie! That would be a great adventure!"

Discussion Questions

1. Do you think King Jeffrey is right? Do you think Princess Isabella fell asleep and dreamed the whole thing? Can you think of any other story where that may have happened? (Hint: the Wizard of Oz) Do you think Princess Isabella will ever see the Leprechaun again?

2. The author of this story tries to help the reader experience the happenings by describing sounds, smells and feelings. Can you give some examples of each:

   -heard   felt -physically
   -smelled   -emotionally

3. Explain how Princess Isabella solved the problem of locating the source of the noise. How did she know which way to go? Would you have been afraid to follow the "click, click, click," noises? Why or why not?

4. Can you give examples of how Princess Isabella showed:

   -Kindness   -Love
   -Responsibility   -Respect

5. Princess Isabella found herself needing to choose between lunch with a leprechaun and getting home in time for lunch. Do you think she chose wisely? What would you have done?

6. Do you think that the more responsible a person is, the more freedom they have? Give an example. Have you ever lost a privilege because you were not responsible?

7. The leprechaun talked with an accent. Did you have trouble sounding out the words? Do you know what country this accent is from? Hint: look in the poem. Do you know anyone who talks with an accent? Where are they from? Do you or someone you know speak a different language? Would you like to learn a different language?

8. While riding under the big oak trees Isabella hear lots of different bird songs. *"That would be worth learning someday,"* she thought to herself. Do you know the difference between different bird sounds? Have you ever thought, "That would be worth learning about someday?" What is it you want to learn more about?

9. The story tells us that Princess Isabella had eyes that showed how she felt on the inside. Can you tell how people feel by looking in their eyes? Can you show the following feelings in your eyes: sleepy, excited, angry, and sad?

Read Our Story - Have Fun Making It Your Own

Adventures of

The Leprechaun

Authors:

Illustrators:

Create Magical Moments
Sharing Together!

Now that you have read and discussed our book

It is time for you to make your book.

Use the following pages to personalize the story:

1. Select the best choice in areas like (He/She). Cross out what you don't want and/or circle what you do want.

2. Name people and animals in your story by filling in the blank (_____) areas.

3. Cross out any parts of the story you don't want and add anything else you do want.

5. As you read the story be aware of pictures in your mind. Sketch in the places provided, pictures about what is happening on each page.

6. Color your illustrations with pencils, crayon, or markers. (Take care that markers don't leak through)

Share Creative Process with Someone you Love!

Introduction

Tell below the story of your story. How is it that you came to create this book. Remember that the quality of the work produced is secondary to the quality of the time you spend together in this relationship building activity. You may wish to include some of the following or other information if you like.

- Child's Age:

- Interests:

- Relationship with Adult: (Grandparent, Teacher, Aunt, etc.)

- Who Did What:

- Notes on Fun Learning Together: Pictures (Optional)

Once upon a time, long, long ago, in a land far away, there lived a beautiful princess/prince named _____. (She/He) lived in a castle, high on a hill, with (his/ her) father, King _____, (his/her) mother, Queen _____, and (her/ his) (little/big) (sister(s)/ brother(s), (Prince/Princess)_____. Often the (Queen Mother/ Duke/Dutchess/Royal Highness), _____, came to visit, and such adventures they had together!

(Suggestion: Draw below the royal family and their castle in the background -See page 4)

_____ had (dark/blonde/brown/red) hair with just a little bit of curl that danced in the wind. Usually, (he/she) kept it tied back, especially when horseback riding. (His/Her) eyes were (dark/light) (brown/ blue/green) had the most amazing ability to show how (he/she) felt on the inside.

On a bright sunny morning (his/her) eyes twinkled with delight as (he/she) took a deep breath and inhaled the sweet smell of lilac bushes that lined the path to the stable. It was a grand morning for a ride in the country and Queen _____ said (he/she) could ride as far as the creek, but needed to be home in time for lunch.

(Can you draw & color below lilac bushes on the way to the stable – see page 5)

As _____ neared the stable (he/she) saw (Mr/Ms) _____ giving the horses grain over the fence. The horses seemed as happy with the sunshine and fresh air as was the little (prince/ princess.)

"Which of your beauties will you be riding today, your highness." asked _____. They were indeed beauties! (He/She) preferred the two white horses, _____ and _____, for a carriage ride, because they not only looked elegant together, but worked as a team, being well paired for the pull. Today she selected _____, a light brown mare, who was gentle, yet enjoyed a good run.

(Mr/Ms) _____ headed toward the barn to get a saddle. Prince/Princess _____ joined him to check on their German Shepard dog _____ and her pups. The sweet smell of hay mixed with other barn smells, some that were not so sweet! Light coming through the windows showed a speckled array of dust in the air.

"Here _____, come puppies," said _____. As (he/she) turned the corner near the last stall (he/she) saw why _____ did not come when called. Like the good mama dog that she was, her first duty was to provide breakfast for her growing family. Reclined in the hay the little fur balls were lined up and happily nursing. (Prince/Princess) _____ snuggled down with them and gently petted _____. The puppies eyes had opened just two days ago and their little faces were so sweet. The littlest one, _____ was having trouble finding a spot to nurse among his brothers and sisters, so (princess/prince) _____ helped him by moving _____ over to make room.

"Now that's better. You must learn to share." (He/She) said.

Just then _____ called, "Ready when you are (prince/princess.)"

(Draw something from the story above. Maybe horses and/or puppies? –see page 6)

"Thanks Jimmy, for your help," said _____ as (he/she) put (his/her) foot in the stirrup to get on _____. The style of (his/her) riding pants looked a bit funny with their pouched-out sides, but they were well designed for comfort in the saddle. (He/ She) headed down the dusty road between the two rows of huge oak trees. The trees were so tall and broad that their branches came together high overhead, shading (him/ her) from the bright morning sun. It was a peaceful ride, interrupted only by the chatter of two chipmunks chasing each other about the branches of a tree. A robin bounced in the short grass, pecking the ground for worms. (He/She) could hear a chorus of other song birds in the area, but really didn't know which bird made which song.

"That would be worth learning someday," _____ thought to (him/her)self. But for today (he/she) was just happy to be right here, enjoying the sights and the sounds of it all.

(Can you draw something from above?...the trees
overhead, chipmunks, birds, etc. -See page 7)

(Prince/Princess) _____ was glad to feel the full warmth again of the sunshine as (he/she) left the trees and entered a meadow. It was like being on a sea, as the grass waved in the wind like waves on an ocean. Sprinkled with an array of wildflowers in hues of blue, yellow and white, the beauty of the meadow beckoned (him/her) to become a part of it. The wind lifted (his/her hair) and _____'s mane. At the same second, both felt the need for speed. They raced across the meadow with a delicious feeling of freedom and joy.

(What do you think the meadow looked like with the
prince/princess riding fast? - See page 8)

Going from a smooth gallop to a trot was bouncy so _____ held tight to _____'s mane.

"Good (boy/girl)," (Princess/ Prince) _____ whispered as they slowed to a walk near the bank of the river. (He/ She) got off (his/her) horse and tied _____ to some large bushes nearby where there was lots of thick grass to munch.

Down the little hill near the water were several large flat rocks that began on the land and went out into the water. This was one of _____ favorite places. (She/He) loved to lay on the rocks in the sunshine and dangle (her/his) toes in the water. It was the perfect spot to study the clouds and imagine what each shape looked like and then watch it change. (He/She) had spent many hours there imagining with her/his grand (father/mother), known to most people as "the (queen mother/Duke/Dutches)," but to Isabella she was "(Grammie/ Grandpa/Aunt /Uncle) _____."

As _____ settled down into (his/her) rock, (she/he) could almost hear (Grand(ma/ pa/aunt/uncle) _____'s voice saying, "be careful near the water." "*I hope (Grammie/ Grandpa/Aunt/Uncle/ Cousin) comes for a visit again soon, "*(she/he) thought with a smile. "*I miss the fun times we have together, and when we get the giggles, and she/he snorts.*"

(Can you see a picture in your mind of what the riverbank looked like? -See page 9)

There were lots of clouds in the sky and the young (prince/princess) identified several cloud creatures including, a fish, rabbit, and bird. The fish was only its mouth, and the rabbit instead of hopping away just made a big slur and was gone. (He/She) could almost hear the bird chirping. No, that sound was not bird like it was more of a clicking sound.

(Draw some pictures of the animal shapes in clouds:
fish, bird, rabbit. Isa's are on page 10)

(Princess/ Prince _____ sat upright to really listen to the unusual sound. Sure enough, it was like, "click, click, click." What was it? Where did it come from? It was too regular to be a twig breaking, and not the kind of fast regular tapping one hears from a woodpecker. What could it be?

(She/He) got up and climbed the bank near the tree and listened. The sound could hardly be heard. So (he/she) went back to the edge of the water. Yes, the sound was louder again there. (She/He) started to walk along the shore to (his/her) right and the sound disappeared, so (he/she) turned and walked in the other direction, and ...yes...definitely, it was getting louder! (His/Her) heart was racing with excitement!

Oh no, it stopped! (The sound that is, not (his/her) heart.) (She/He) stopped too, waiting, and listening. There seemed to be another sound now. Almost like a hum. Not like a bee would hum, or even a humming bird kind of sound, but almost like a voice far away humming. Ever so quietly she crept forward. Yes, it was getting louder.

(Can you draw a picture of the princess/princess trying
find the sound? – Ours is on page 11)

By this time (Princess/Prince) _____had traveled quite a distance along the bank of the river. It was more like a stream at this point. There were rocks and a big log so that anyone could even cross to the other side. And that's exactly what (he/she) decided to do. (He/She) planned (his/her) path carefully, which rock each step would take until using the log to cross the stream. (She/He) knew that even if (he/she) fell in, it was not very deep. Just as (she/he) stepped foot on the far side of the river (she/he) heard another strange sound. Like someone clearing their throat, and then a little cough. (He/She) looked around and at first couldn't see anything unusual. But then (he/she) saw him, and unusual only began to describe the sight (she/he) saw.

(Try to draw a picture of the prince/princess crossing the stream. See page 12)

It was no wonder (he/she) hadn't seen him right away because he was only a few feet high, and he was dressed in green so blended in with the green grass and bushes. He sat on a rock a few feet away from where (she/he) stood, and was looking right at (him/her.) He was shorter than _____ little (brother/sister/cousin) _____, but was not a child, but a man. His skin was wrinkled and he had a beard. His clothes were different, to say the least. His shoes had gold buckles and the toes came to a point and curled up over his foot. He wore long stockings and short pants, banded just below the knee and held tight with a gold button. He had a vest with a pocket watch and a tailored jacket and a top-hat with a brown band and gold buckle that held something green in it. Just as (she/he) realized that something was like a clover leaf, the hat started moving.

He tipped it to (him/her) and said, "Top of the mornin' to ye (lad/lass.)"

(Draw what you think the leprechaun looked like. See page 13)

"Oh my", said the little (princess/prince), quite in shock. "Who are you"?

He got up from where he sat on the rock, did a deep bow and answered with a poem....

"Why, I'm Patrick, Dennis, Michael O'Shaun
     An Irish elf, called a leprechaun,
   Dressed in green from my head to my toes
     For that is the color of leprechaun clothes.
     .... and just who might ye be,
        Yon, (pretty/handsome) (lad/lassie) wee?
     Are ye gone, and lost from home,
       In these woods, so far to roam?"

"I, ah, ...I am (P-Princess/P-Prince) _____ (she/he) said with a tremble in (her/his) voice. "I heard s-something and c-came looking for the s-sound," (he/she) stammered.

The elf pulled on his whiskers and asked, "Aye, what sorta sound then?"

"Oh, it was first a click, click, click sound and then a humming sound", (prince/princess) _____ said, feeling a little more comfortable, now that he wasn't talking in verse anymore. *"He does have a strange accent though," (she/he)* thought to (herself/himself).

(Can you picture what it looked like talking to a leprechaun? See page 14)

"Aye, I'm a bettin' what ye heard was me wee hammer a tappin', and I'm lik'in to hum to meself whilst workin'. Actually, I was takin' a wee bit of a break from me workin' and just a hummin'."

(Princess/Prince) _____ thought, " *Yep it must have been him I heard.*" *(His/Her)* thoughts were interrupted by hearing him clear his throat again and asking rather formally, "Was 'bout to have a wee bit of lunch (lad/lass,) would ye share a bit with me then?"

"Oh lunch, Oh no, I have to be home for lunch!" _____ said as (he/she) turned to leave and then remembered (his/her) manners. "Thank you so much for the kind invitation, but I really don't have time today. May I come again another time?"

(What would the Princess/Princess look like leaving the leprechaun? See page 15)

(Prince/Princess) _____ glanced up to the sun high in the sky and knew it was close to lunch time. (She/He) quickly, but carefully, crossed the tiny river and ran along the beach until (his/her) favorite rocks were in sight. (Her/His) horse, _____ was enjoying the tall grass, but glad when the little (prince/princess) untied the reigns and swung into the saddle. The ride home was like a race to keep (his/her) promise to be home in time for lunch. Queen _____ and/or king _____ gave (Prince/Princess) a lot a freedom for (his/her) age because _____ was responsible. (He/she) did (his/her) chores and was careful, and honest, and kind. The little (Prince/Princess) knew that if she was not true to (his/her) word, to be home in time for lunch, some of the trust and freedom (he/she) enjoyed might be taken away. Her little (brother/sister) _____, didn't have so much freedom because (he/she) was several years younger, and wasn't capable of earning trust yet.

(He/She) couldn't help but think of (his/her) other invitation. *"How interesting it would be to have lunch with a leprechaun"*, (he/she) thought. *"Oh, what if I am late. Surely mom and dad will understand if I tell them about Patrick Dennis Michael O'Shaun."*

(Prince/Princess) _____ was thankful that (Mr/Ms) _____ was there to care for _____ when (she/he) reached the stables. (His/Her) legs carried (him/her) swiftly to the castle where (she/he) stopped for a quick wash. (He/She) really should change clothes, but there probably wasn't time.

Cook gave (him/her) a nod saying, "Best hurry dear, there is to be a special guest for lunch." *"Oh no!"* thought _____, *"Not one of those very prim and proper lords or ladies. I'll be in trouble for wearing my riding clothes."*

(Pick out something on this page to draw. We chose the cook. See page 16)

As _____ entered the dining room (she/he) saw (his/her) (mom/dad) (King/Queen) _____, who smiled warmly beaconing (him/her) in.

"Whew, that's a relief." thought _____.

"You made it back just in time (sweetheart/son/daughter)" said (King/Queen) _____ "come and be seated." Just as (Prince/Princess) _____ started to ask about the special guest, who walked in but (Queen Mother/ Grandpa/ Aunt/ Uncle) _____.

(Prince/Princess) _____ ran to (him/her) with arms outstretched saying, "Oh _____ I'm so glad to see you!" Their hugs were always warm and long. Little (brother/sister) _____ joined in a group hug.

"How long can you stay asked _____.

"Long enough for some great adventures" was (his/her) (Grandmother's/ grandfather's/ aunt's/ uncle's) reply with a twinkle in (his/her) eye.

(Can you picture that "group hug"? See page 17)

After hugs were shared all around, the family settled for lunch. King _____ asked _____ if (he/she) would like to say the blessing. The family held hands and bowed their heads, as the little (prince/princess) thanked God not only for the food, but also the beautiful day and for family and friends. Their tasty lunch of ham biscuits, potato salad and applesauce was enjoyed as they visited together. When the conversation got around to what _____ had been doing that morning (she/he) at first hesitated. But then shared (his/her) ride to the rocks, and hearing the clicking, and then how exciting it was to meet a leprechaun.

King _____ said, "Now _____, isn't that the place by the river where you lay and look at the clouds and sometimes fall asleep?"

"Well sometimes," (he/she) admitted.

"And don't you think that maybe meeting the leprechaun might have just been a dream?"

"Oh no, daddy," the little (Prince/Princess) replied, "He was real. And he even asked me to lunch, but I couldn't stay, because I promised to be home for lunch, ...and he invited me to come back another time.

"Oh, that's nice honey," said (his/her) mom with a wink at (his/her) dad.

"(Grammie/Grandpa, Auntie/ Uncle) _____, you believe me, don't you?" pleaded _____.

"Of course I do sweetheart," (he/she) replied, "Do you suppose I could go with you when you go back to see him again?"

"Oh, yes (Grammie/ Grandpa/ Auntie/ Uncle)! That would be a great adventure!

(What do you see as the last scene in this adventure. See page 18)

Discussion Questions

1. Do you think King_____is right? Do you think (Prince/Princess)_____ fell asleep and dreamed the whole thing? Can you think of any other story where that may have happened? (Hint: The Wizard of Oz) Do you think Princess Isabella will ever see the Leprechaun again?

2. The author of this story tries to help the reader experience the happenings by describing sounds, smells and feelings. Can you give some examples of each:

   -heard   felt -physically

   -smelled   -emotionally

3. Explain how(Prince/ Princess) Isabella solved the problem of locating the source of the Noise. How did (he/she) know which way to go? Would you have been afraid to follow the "click, click, click," noises? Why or why not?

4. Can you give examples of how (Princes/ Princess) _____ showed:

   -Kindness   -Love

   -Responsibility   -Respect

5. (Princess/Princess) _____ found (herself/himself) needing to choose between lunch with a leprechaun and getting home in time for lunch. Do you think (he/she) chose wisely? What would you have done?

6. Do you think that the more responsible a person is, the more freedom they have? Give an example. Have you ever lost a privilege because you were not responsible?

7. The leprechaun talked with an accent. Did you have trouble sounding out the words? Do you know what country this accent is from? Hint: look in the poem. Do you know anyone who talks with an accent? Where are they from? Do you or someone you know speak a different language? Would you like to learn a different language?

8. While riding under the big oak trees _____ hear lots of different bird songs. *"That would be worth learning someday,"* (he/she) thought to (her/himself). Do you know the difference between different bird sounds? Have you ever thought, "That would be worth learning about someday?" What is it you want to learn more about?

9. The story tells us that (Prince/Princess) _____ had eyes that showed how (he/she) felt on the inside. Can you tell how people feel by looking in their eyes? Can you show the following feelings in your eyes: sleepy, excited, angry, and sad?

Questions / Evaluation
(Optional)

1. What did you learn from discussing the questions after reading about Princess Isabella?

2. Put _X_ in front of the things you liked about creating your personalized book?

    Put _O_ in front of the things you did not like.

    ____ being in the story

    ____ having my family and/or friends in the story with me

    ____ naming the animals

    ____ getting to know better the person I worked with in making this book

    ____ having fun with the person making this book with me

    ____ drawing the pictures

    ____ coloring the pictures

    ____ reading my story to others after it was finished

    ____ other: _____

3. Could you see pictures in your mind of what was happening in the story?

4. Could you draw those pictures on the paper?

5. What was the most exciting part of the story for you?

6. What do you think happens next in the story?

7. How do you think this total experience could be improved?

If you would like to share your thoughts

contact Linda:
rlromblom@frontier.com

About the Authors/Illustrators

The Adventures of Princess Isabella – The Leprechaun

This book began as bedtime stories told by a grandmother (Linda Romblom) to her granddaughter (Isabella Walker), who became the leading character, Princess Isabella in their adventures. Her family members and friends play supporting roles and she named animals in the story as it was told.

As Isabella grew and became interested in reading and drawing, these special times between grandmother and granddaughter expanded into creating this book. Their time together was so wonderful that they came up with a way to "share the magic!" They added a template to the back of the book so others can personalize the story with their own character names and create artwork together. Questions that help readers relate the story to their lives and talk about important issues were also added to enrich the bonding experience.

Linda Romblom, primary author, was assisted by Isabella in saying things in a way her friends would understand. Isabella Walker, primary illustrator, encouraged Grammie Linda to not only help with coloring, but occasionally try her hand at drawing.

Linda has a master degree in education, and prior to her recent retirement taught Family and Consumer Science to high school students, including course work in Child Development. This book incorporates many of the foundational principles she used in lesson planning that enhance cognitive development and creativity in children.

Isabella is a second grade student who enjoys a wide range of extracurricular activities including: Brownie Girl Scouts, basketball, soccer, karate, and music (both violin and piano). She loves horses and dogs, especially German Shepherds. Isabella brings a delightful child's perspective to the language and artwork of this unique together project.

CPSIA information can be obtained
at www.ICGtesting.com
Printed in the USA
FSOW04n0410020317
31409FS